Kathleen Kirkland

NINETY SEVEN DAYS

Table of Contents

Copyright

Text copyright © 2020 by Kath Kirkland ISBN: Paperback – 978-1-9163035-2-2

The first edition published in December 2015.

Updated edition published in July 2020.

Chapter One

Sunday 15th April

David was numb; he had never felt this numb ever, or indeed so alone in his whole life. He sat down on the sofa with his head in his hands as if this was to ease his sorrow and he cried like a baby. Just as a baby cries because he is hungry, David was hungry right now, hungry for his Wife. Fifteen years of marriage, stripped from him, gone in a heartbeat. 'Why?' He blabbed. 'Why did it happen so quickly, she seemed fine?' He sat wiping his tears on his sleeve, the very same sleeve that his Wife Joan had ironed only three weeks previous. Fear struck him again. 'How am I going to cook, I have no idea how to use the cooker or the microwave?' David's tears were now falling onto his shoe's, the same shoes that Joan spent hours polishing for him each Sunday evening. 'I am lost, I can't cook, Adam will go hungry and he will starve to death.' Irrational thoughts were now filling his head, coming thick and fast. Adam was their only son; he was a strapping lad and a very mature twelve years old who aspires to be a doctor one day. Adam is a blue-eyed boy and the centre of Joan's world, as she was told when she was younger that she would be unable to have children ever and that broke her heart, just as David's heart was feeling right now. So, when Joan found out that she was carrying she was thrilled beyond control and cherished every day with Adam. Adam was extremely handsome and Joan and He always joked that he will break many hearts when he is older, with his bright blue eyes, blond hair and gorgeous looks. Adam never wanted for anything, not that he was spoilt or anything, it was just that Joan was so grateful for the blessing of his life that it meant she made sure he did not want for anything. Nothing was too much trouble for Joan, he remembered the Christmas before last, she had worked so many hours overtime, which enabled her to buy Adam the computer he wanted. David would never have spent a quarter of the price Joan did on his machine, but Adam wanted it so much, that Joan without hesitation worked to afford it. David recalled the delight on Adam's face that Christmas morning when he opened the huge box. He was so thankful and he showed his appreciation with lots of affection. Adam is such an affectionate boy, which was a trait that he inherited from Joan without a doubt. Now it was left to David to provide all the affection for both Joan and him. Fear struck him again, how is he going to be a good father and at the same time be a great mother?

Adam went to Joan's sister, Elanor, on the day Joan was taken into the hospice and has been there ever since. David was immensely thankful; he would have hated Adam seeing him in floods of tears every five minutes. Also, there was a funeral to arrange, he did not want Adam being subjected to such horrors, not at his age. Fear struck David again, the hospice said that he must make an appointment with the registry office to register Joan's death and obtain a death certificate. The same registry office they were married at fifteen years earlier. Tears started falling down his face again, just like a water-full unable to stop, remembering the water-full they stood under in Jamaica where they renewed their wedding vows last summer. 'Was it going to be like this all the time?' David howled, 'Everything I do, reminding me of things that Joan and I did together?' David almost jumped out of his skin at the sound of the doorbell. 'Oh no who can that be, please I cannot speak to anyone now.' David muttered to himself as he shuffled towards the front door when he opened it he was slightly relieved to see Sandra the social worker from the hospice standing there with a huge smile on her face. Wiping away his tears on his sleeve, he smiled, nodded and beckoned Sandra to enter. Sandra was a very rotund lady and her coat managed to cover her curves, which was a shame as her curves matched her vivacious character. He remembered Joan saying that she was very much passed retirement age, but carried on working at the hospice as she loved her job and he was thankful right now for this.

'David, I'm glad you are here. I know it's a silly question, but how are you feeling?' Sandra answered her question with the pained expression on her face.

'Numb, just numb.' Tears started rolling again, this time onto the perfectly polished wooden floor.

'I am sure it is, please if you ever need someone to talk to you know my office door is always open. We don't just care for the patients you know; we support the bereaved also darling.' Sandra placed a reassuring hand on David's shoulder. Sandra was a lively character from the East End of London and called everyone darling.

David almost smiled. 'Thank you, I appreciate it.

Did you just come to see how I am?' He enquired.

Sandra smiled, 'Yes and no.'

'Oh?' David looked confused.

'I have a letter for you. Joan had written it and taken it with her in her bag to the hospice. She gave strict instructions to me and the other staff that it was only to be passed onto to you once she was no longer with us. She asked that I stay with you whilst you read it.' Sandra took the envelope from her handbag and handed it to David. The envelope smelt of Joan, it was her favourite perfume, the perfume he had brought from the duty-free shop after his last business trip to.

'Shall I put the kettle on?' Sandra walked towards the kitchen before she heard a reply.

'That would be lovely, only I have no idea where anything is in the kitchen?' David shouted after her, whilst staring at the letter he had just been given, cradling it as if it was made of expensive china.

'Don't worry.' Sandra yelled. 'Women are all the same, where they put things. One kitchen is almost identical to another.' Sandra reassured him from the inside of a cupboard. 'Tea or coffee?' A muffled sound from came from the

Kitchen under the sound of open and shut doors.

'Coffee, white with two sugars please.' David let out a muffled reply as he continued to stare at the envelope. The handwriting, it was Joan's best handwriting, written using her favourite Mont Blanc fountain pen, the one he had brought her several Christmases ago, the fountain pen she so longed for.

Sandra returned with two hot steaming mugs of coffee. 'There you go. Have you opened it yet?' Sandra quizzed whilst placing the two mugs on the coffee table.

'No, I am afraid to. Why has she written me a letter before she died?' David asked looking confused.

'Well, you won't know until you open it.' Sandra looked at the envelope.

'Did she tell you what was in it?' David asked, still focusing on the envelope and not Sandra.

'No, sorry, I have no idea? Joan's instructions were for me to hand-deliver the envelope to you, soon after her passing. So here I am and it is not the strangest request I have ever had.' Sandra said blowing her coffee to cool it down.

'Oh.' David did now turn his attention to Sandra.

Sandra waved the comment away, 'do you wish to open it alone?' asked.

'No, I don't think I can open it at all if the truth is known. Sandra, can you open it for me?' Throwing the envelope into Sandra's hands as if it were a hot potato.

'If you are sure, gladly I will.' Sandra carefully opened the envelope seal, being cautious not to tear any of the envelope that was so beautifully handcrafted. Inside she could see a pretty pink flowered paper, which she delicately removed and unfolded the letter, which was equally as beautifully written. Sandra handed the letter to David; he shook his head violently and waved his hand to gesture that Sandra read it.

Chapter Two

To my darling David

I am sorry that you are reading this letter now, as it means that I have passed to the other side and no longer with you in the body. Please be assured that I will be with you forever in spirit. Firstly, I must thank Sandra for bringing this letter to you. She is a lovely lady, nothing too much trouble for anyone. Now David, please don't be angry with me, but when I knew in January, I knew that I was dying. The consultant told me two weeks after Christmas that I only have three months left to live. Cancer had invaded every organ in my body and there was nothing they could do to change that. Maybe one day when our son is a fine Doctor that he so aspires to be he can create a cure for this hideous disease. During my time off, I have been busy preparing for my death. It may sound rather morbid, but I knew it was imminent, so I thought I would make myself useful and organise Adam and yourself, as you know how much I love organising. I need you to go into the loft, yes, the loft. What is up there you are wondering; well I will tell you what to look for? The favourite red suitcase of mine, the one that I used on our anniversary trip two years ago, you need to bring it downstairs as inside the suitcase is all you need to know. I will sign off by telling you how sorry I am for not telling you, but I didn't want my final days with you my darling husband and our gorgeous son spent moping around wondering when the inevitable was going to happen, and you telling me to sit down every time I coughed or sneezed. Please forgive me, as I know you will find it in your heart to. Please do not tell Adam about the contents of this letter, I would hate him to think I had lied to him. He has still never forgiven me for lying to him about Father Christmas! This is a bigger lie than a man in a red suit visiting him on Christmas Eve and bringing him presents. I have enjoyed our marriage; it was amazing and I could not have asked for a better man to share my life with. I fell in love with your gorgeous blue eyes and boyish good looks all them years ago and in my eye's you have never changed. You were always there for me during times of sadness and of course, we shared many, many happy times and for that, I am eternally grateful. I understand you will miss me, but please believe me that I am in no pain now and will always be with you and Adam watching out for you so that no harm comes to either of you. I love you.

Joan. XXXXXXXXXXXXXXX (one kiss for every year of marriage).

Sandra looked up and tears were rolling down her cheek, she tried to wipe them before David noticed, but his eyes were flooded and he probably wasn't even aware of her tears.

David broke the silence. 'That's my Joan. Thoughtful until the end, she always did think of absolutely everything, every last final detail.' Wiping the tears from his face with his sleeve.

'Well she hasn't let you down this time, has she?' Sandra tried to break a smile. 'So, are you going to get up into the loft as Joan has asked?'

'Yes of course.' David stood up from the sofa but almost lost his balance and had to hold on to the arm of the sofa to regain control of his legs, this was certainly too much to take in on one day. 'Please follow me.' David gestured to Sandra to follow him towards the loft hatch. They both stood and stared at the ceiling where the loft opening was, both wondering what secret lies up there, that Joan had planned.

Chapter Three

The loft always gave David the creeps. It had a musky smell, felt extremely cold and vacant. David opened the hatch, pulled down the ladders and climbed the rickety ladder into the abyss above the house. David let out a pained yelp.

'What is it darling are you hurt?' Sandra shouted apprehensively.

'It's OK, I am fine thanks, just a shock that's all and it's here.'

'What is up there?' Sandra wished at this moment in time, she did not have a phobia of ladders and wish she could have been up there too.

'The suitcase Joan mentioned in her letter, the red one and it has a huge translucent bow tied around it.' David was fighting the tears. 'Hang on, there is a silver gift tag attached.' David couldn't bring himself to relay the wording to Sandra once he had read it.

David, this is the closest colour I could find to crystal for fifteen years of a happy marriage. XX.

'Are you going to pass it down to me, or are you wanting to open it up, up there?' Sandra didn't want to harass David but knew he should not be alone right now.

'I'll pass it down, but please be careful it is very heavy, I have no idea why it is so heavy.' David positioned the red suitcase over the hatch and slowly manoeuvred it down the ladder. The weight of the suitcase took Sandra by surprise as she caught it and almost dropped it at the same time.

'Gosh you are right; it is very heavy?' Sandra was now admiring the bow that had been tied neatly around the case. David descended the ladder and brushed his clothing down, attempting to remove all the cobwebs and dust that had clung to him in the short space of time that he was in the loft. They both stood deadly still and in total silence looking at the red suitcase for what seemed like hours. Sandra was the first to break the silence. 'Now what?' Not really what David wanted to hear.

'Open it I suppose. That is what Joan asked for.'

David remarked, still staring at the red suitcase.

'Shall we carry it downstairs together then?'

Sandra questioned but David didn't appear to be listening. 'Do you want me to carry it down darling?'

'What if I don't want to see the contents? What if it was better left in the loft? What have I done?' David rambled.

'Joan gave me strict instructions that you must read the letter after she had passed. She went to all this trouble for you, do you imagine there is something so awful in there?' Sandra felt like a nag.

'You are right, sorry, how silly of me. Yes, let us take it downstairs and if you don't mind sticking around for a few more minutes whilst I open this, I may need some moral support.' David mumbled.

'Of course, I'll put the kettle on again darling, we may need it.' Sandra descended the stairs with David following behind, both struggling to manoeuvre the heavy case.

'It is heavy I'll give it that if nothing else.' David muttered to himself as he struggled with the suitcase.

'How on earth did she get it up there?'

'Maybe she filled it up whilst it was up there?' Sandra suggested.

'Of course, she did, she was always the logical one.' David was nodding frantically.

Sandra appeared from the kitchen with another two hot mugs of coffee to see David still staring blankly at the red suitcase.

'Well, it won't open itself, David.' Sandra said whilst sipping her hot coffee. 'Come on, you can't put it off forever.' Sandra encouraged.

David took a seat on the edge of the sofa and shuffled the suitcase nearer to him. He removed the bow that was so delightfully tied around the red suitcase. He took a huge intake of air as if he was about to throw himself out of an aircraft. 'Here goes.' David announced and unclipped the catches. He closed his eyes and as he opened the red suitcase, as he was unable to look inside.

Chapter Four

'Another letter, gosh this is like a treasure hunt. She always did enjoy games.' David spoke through gritted teeth, almost cursing Joan's enthusiasm. David opened the letter delicately so not to rip any of the envelope.

Dear David

Thank you for opening the red suitcase. I bet it took you ages to decide whether to open it or not. Well, I am glad you have. Please don't worry yourself, there is nothing ghastly in here, all that is in here are things that will help you carry on without me. I am so sorry my Darling that I am not here with you right now. I have been writing a diary of my final months and all the activities I have been up to. As you read through the diaries, it will hopefully make sense. Please, only open the folders and albums when it tells you to do so in the diaries, otherwise, the messages may get muddled. I am sorry again, please forgive me, but I couldn't see you struggle on without my help, even if I am not here with you now. I have considered every aspect of life, to try and make it as painless as possible for you.

I love you David XX.

'What an earth does she mean?' David wiped his brow. 'Activities, when did she get a chance to carry out activities?' David wept again.

'Well, maybe it will all become clearer when you read her diaries?' Sandra finished her coffee and placed it on the coffee table.

'I cannot read her diaries, they are personal.' David sat shaking his head.

'But she has asked you to, she went to all the effort with the suitcase for you.' Sandra rested her hand on his shoulder. 'Shall I leave you alone. This is a personal thing between Joan and you, not something you need to share with me.' Sandra got up to leave.

'Sandra please wait a minute; I just want to say thank you for everything. I wouldn't have had the courage to open the case alone.' David held out his hand to shake Sandra's.

'Please if you need me for any reason, do let me know darling. You have my number. Enjoy the diaries and I hope you find out what all the activities that Joan was up to before she passed.' Sandra removed her coat from the hook, put it on but didn't fasten it. She opened the door and let herself out. David was still standing staring at the red suitcase. He stood staring at the suitcase for what seemed like hours, it must have been some time as the daylight outside was slowly disappearing for the day. He was exhausted and laid on the sofa to rest his head before he realised it was morning.

Chapter Five

The sun was shining brightly through the undrawn curtains of the living room. 'Joan will be mad with me for not drawing the curtains.' He muttered to himself. Then reality set in that Joan was no longer with him. He rose from the sofa and accidentally kicked the red suitcase that was still in the middle of the floor. 'Damn.' He yelled in pain. He had forgotten about the suitcase. 'I will have to read the contents now I suppose, I can't keep it sitting there in the middle of the living room for much longer.' He picked up his mobile phone, noticing the battery was almost flat from not being charged for many hours. There were fifteen text messages and nineteen voicemails from concerned friends and family. He threw the phone onto the sofa in temper and climbed the stairs for a well-deserved shower. He questioned himself every step of the way. 'What was in those diaries?' He was inquisitive to read them but anxious at the same time.

The shower was hot, hotter than he had ever managed to stand under before. He was almost trying to burn his skin as if he was trying to self-inflict pain. Once he had showered and dressed and walked downstairs into the living room and sat staring at the red suitcase again. 'Oh, Joan.' He cried out in pain. 'Why did you have to be so secretive?' He started thumping his fist onto the coffee table in anger. Not being able to torment himself any longer he lifted the first book out of the suitcase and opened it to page one.

Chapter Six

Monday 8th January

Dear David

I am writing this diary so that after I have passed away you can read my thoughts running up to that awful day that lies ahead of me. Today I got the number 42 bus to the hospital, just in case anyone saw my car parked at the hospital and started asking questions. At least on the bus, I can say I am off shopping. I saw my consultant, a lovely chap, Doctor Harvey, he is very young and very handsome. I hope our Adam makes it as a doctor when he is older as he aspires to. I didn't hear anything that came out of the doctor's mouth, not that I was in awe of him or anything, just I was unable to hear any words. I could see his mouth moving, but there didn't seem to be any sound coming from there. After he said the fateful word 'TERMINAL' I just shut off. I have the greatest ability to do that, it drives you mad at times doesn't it David? You say I am not there in the room with you, but of course, I am, I am just switched off from the outside world, transformed in my thoughts. It is an art I have developed over the years living with two men. Adam and you can both talk the arse of a donkey and most of the time at the same time, each fighting for my attention, I then have to switch off and not listen to either of you. It is the easiest way, to be cruel to be kind and all that, otherwise one of you gets the attention and the other gets offended. Even you David at your age, you do get offended if I give my attention to Adam when you are also trying to talk to me. So, there you go David, all these years you have wondered why I did what I did thinking it was to annoy you both, but it wasn't, it was so I did not offend either of you. I do hope you can forgive me. Anyway, back to the consultant. I had a scan just after Christmas as I had symptoms that our lovely doctor suspected was cancer and I was in severe pain most of the time. The appointment was to get the results of the scan I had a couple of weeks previously. He sat me down and turned to me and spoke very softly and sincere. 'It's not good news Mrs Jones I am afraid.' He said. 'I suspected as much. Just tell me how it is, no beating around the bush, treading on eggshells and all that rubbish.' I ordered him to tell me. 'It is terminal I am afraid, Joan.' The Doctor sat looking at me with sincere eyes. That was it. I didn't hear anything after that moment. He was talking as I could see his mouth and hands moving in time, just I couldn't understand anything he was saying. It was almost as if he was talking in a foreign language. 'Joan do you have any questions?' Doctor Harvey asked. I felt embarrassed that I hadn't heard a word he said, I was afraid to ask him something he had already told me, so I just asked 'How long?' Just like that, although he knew what I meant. 'It is always hard to put a definitive date on these things, I wish we had a crystal ball.' The doctor rambled. 'Doctor, please how long?' I urged. 'I would estimate three months, maybe more, but also very probably maybe less. Please is there anything else you wish to ask me?' The Doctor still had the sincere look on his face. I shook my head, shook his hand and thanked him for his time and gathered my things in a rather untidily manner and left his consulting room. Once outside the Consultants room, I was almost disabled unable to move from where I was standing, frozen on the spot. A nurse saw me leave Doctor Harvey's room and quickly grabbed me before I fell to the floor. 'Would you like a cup of tea?' She asked kindly. I shook my head but said 'Yes please.' It was only when I was on the bus later, I realised how stupid I must have looked. She sat me in a side room and asked if I had just been given some bad news. She had picked many a poor person up from the floor after leaving the Doctor's consulting room. She asked if she could call someone for me; a family member or a friend. I explained that no one knows I am here and I wanted to keep it that way for now. She respected my decision. Once I had finished my tea, I thanked her immensely and left for the bus stop. I was grateful at this moment that I had left the car at home, as I was in no fit state to drive a car. The sleet was falling hard from the sky and it dawned on me at that moment that this is the last winter I will have to suffer. No

David was sobbing harder than he had ever sobbed. 'Joan, why did you not tell anyone? You should never have gone through this alone.'

Chapter Seven

David, sat at his desk and logged on to his emails, but was unable to concentrate. He picked up Joan's diary and started reading again.

Tuesday 9th January

I telephoned work today, as I wasn't able to face going in. I had the day off yesterday, I told them I had a Doctor's appointment. They asked if everything was okay? I brushed them off, with women's problems. Grace answered the phone and I told her I was suffering from a migraine. It wasn't a lie, as I did have a headache, after the news I learnt yesterday. Grace was sympathetic, suffering from migraine's herself. She started telling me about a new herbal remedy she has started taking for migraines, but it can take four or five months to start working. I thanked her kindly. What I wanted to say is, 'thanks Grace, but I have only got a few months left to live.' I explained that hopefully, I will be back tomorrow. I had a lie-down, trying to process the conversation I just had with Grace and decided to cook you and Adam's favourite dinner, Lasagna. When you came home, you were concerned about my headache, as you hadn't seen me since yesterday morning when you left for work.

David remembered her headache; the pain must have been unbearable. He continued reading.

Wednesday 10th January

I still couldn't face work, to be honest, I have no idea what I am going to do. I want to carry on as if everything is normal, but I am also unsure of how I can. The postman knocked with a parcel for next door. We chatted for a few minutes, (well, he chatted mostly) he asked if we had any holidays planned later in the year. I shrugged him off, with a 'we are looking into something', questions that under normal circumstances would be easy to answer, but now.

David dropped the diary to the floor and cried. 'Why didn't you tell me?'

Thursday 11th January

Today I had an appointment with our lovely Doctor, to discuss the results of my scan. There was no good news that the Doctor could give me, only that she will support me, providing me with pain relief when I need it.

Friday 12th January

I sat and sobbed today. I tried to think of ways I could tell you. I couldn't think of an easy way to bring the subject up in conversation, without it being a shock. I played over several different conversations in my head on how to tell you. For the moment, I need to think about the best way to tell you.

Sunday 15th January

The weekend went by quite normally; you working on your laptop, Adam on his gaming computer and myself, curled up on the sofa with a novel. I wonder if I will finish the novel before I pass? Will I die, not knowing the ending? I then started to think about how many other people have been in the same situation? We have had many relatives return books to the library, for their family members that have passed, but I have never given it a thought that they may not have finished it. It reminded me of an episode of Hancock's Half Hour, where he borrows a book from a library and the last page is missing and he doesn't find out the ending to the story. It did make me chuckle. I decided I would search up the episode and watch it during the week.

David closed the diary, he struggled to understand how Joan was so jovial.

Chapter Eight

The microwave sounded out a loud ping to notify David that his frozen meal was ready. He removed the hot plastic gourmet meal of chilli con Carne and chose to eat it from the carton to save on the washing up. Once he sat at the kitchen table, he opened Joan's diary to read some more. Burning himself on the contents of the chilli he soon realised he had cooked it for many more minutes than the packet had recommended.

Monday 16th January

I have been pondering for days now how to tell you, David, please believe me. How do you tell your Husband of fifteen years and your only Son, that you have been told by your consultant that you possibly have three months left to live or maybe less or maybe even more? So, I have decided not to tell either of you. I am just going to get on with things as normal so not to make the last few months a living fear that each day is my last. My first concern is the fact that you have no idea how any of the appliances in this housework; dishwasher, washing machine, cooker, microwave, vacuum cleaner and possibly even more. What I have done is collated all the instruction manuals to all the appliances and placed them in the blue folder inside the red suitcase, labelled 'manuals. I hope this helps, I am just sorry I couldn't show you before I passed, but then you would have suspected something. It then dawned on me that you would not have time to clean the house regularly, so I decided to find a cleaner or housemaid for you. Not knowing how to find one, I went to the Jobcentre to investigate. I spoke to an assistant (or whatever they call themselves) who was extremely helpful and sympathetic. I told her my exact plans and she helped me no end to put together a job specification. She was rather embarrassed about the question asking when the vacancy will be available from, she just smiled and she said 'We can leave that one blank for now.' I thanked her very much. She assured me the job advert would be up within a few days and I can start interviewing. I hadn't thought of that part of the task in hand, interviewing! I am sure there is nothing to it, just judge my instincts and go with that. Once I have found a suitable candidate to take over the running of our house, I can provide the details, but as yet the vacancy has not been advertised, so at this point, I cannot. I am glad we never had to 'sign on', it is the most awful place I have ever visited and all the Staff in that place had a look of fear on their faces when anyone walked through the door. The doors are manned by a huge muscled security guard. David, that I am eternally grateful for, never having to subject ourselves to that place. Once I returned home, I took a little nap before I prepared dinner and you came home from work.

    David felt as though his wife was cheating on him, being deceitful, but she had her reasons, for that he didn't fully understand. He was afraid to read on any further, wondering what else she had arranged single-handed.

Chapter Nine

David woke and it took a few moments to realise why the bed was empty. He then remembered Joan's diaries that were on the bedside table. He picked up the diary and started to read on.

Tuesday 16th January

Wow, what a shock opening my emails this morning was. Several people have replied already to my job advert. None of the applicants so far are suitable; one has a bad back and unable to bend, another is allergic to household dust. The assistant at the jobcentre did say, that there may be several applicants that are not suitable but not to be put off by the process. I closed my laptop and decided, I will look again in a few days.

Wednesday 17th January

I went back to work today, although I am still not sure I should be there. I told the girls I still had a migraine, using that as an excuse as to why I am not my normal cheery self. Grace, asked me quietly when we were alone if everything was okay at home. I snapped at her, for thinking such a thing. Grace was upset by my outburst. I apologised, explaining that I still had a migraine. She gave me some of her herbal remedy, which I took gratefully. The area manager, Nigel, came in and called me into a meeting, which I was really worried about. I suspected it was due to all the time I have had off. I hoped they were not considering sacking me. If they were, I would have to have told them about my situation, surely there are rules, about not being able to sack a dying woman. Thankfully, it was a conversation about redundancy. I sighed a huge sigh of relief, which took Nigel by surprise. I explained that I thought I was being sacked. We both laughed about it. He said I am a valid member of staff and he will be sorry to see me go if I decide to take the offer. Nigel explained that the council are making some job cuts and everyone has been asked if they would consider redundancy. The other girls have been asked, but they were told not to tell me. I am going to accept the offer, but I didn't want to seem too keen in the meeting, so asked for a couple of days to consider the offer, as it was a shock to me.

Thursday 18th January

I found the episode of Hancock's Half Hour, the one with the missing last page of the library book. It did make me laugh out loud.

Friday 19th January

I found several old comedies, I haven't seen for ages; Monty Python, Morecambe and Wise, The Two Ronnie's and Bless This House.

Chapter Ten

David struggled to untangle the cord from the vacuum cleaner and started to cry, tears of shame more than anything, mortified that he was clueless how to unravel a chord on a basic appliance. He threw the plug at the wall, which left a perfect three-pin imprint just above the skirting board and then he gave up and retired to the comfort of the sofa and there lying on the coffee table was Joan's diary. After much deliberation, he picked it up and read some more.

Saturday 20th January

You wanted to go and buy some paint as you decided that the living room could do with a spruce up. There wasn't any conversation, as to whether I was coming along, as we always do things together. So, we wandered around the D.I.Y shop, looking at the colours of paint. It was a joint decision on which colour looked the best and would suit the living room. This seemed irrelevant to me as I would not see it for much longer. I decided on a colour, just so we could get out of the shop and I could get home. I am sorry David, that I chose that colour and it may not be the best choice. This is why I made my mind up so quickly when normally I am so indecisive.

David sat staring at the paint on the wall, that had only been there a few months. He did like it after he had painted it, although he wasn't sure of the colour on the tin. Now every time he looks at the wall, he will remember that day. He decided, once he is feeling better, he will repaint it.

Sunday 21st January

You woke up early, ready with your paintbrush in hand. You muttered a lot of swear words that day, you wished you hadn't started to redecorate.

Monday 22nd January

I had a meeting with the management at work, to tell them I am willing to accept the redundancy. I played down how reluctant I was. He told me that he will have the paperwork drawn up, ready for me to sign tomorrow. How sad, to leave the job I love so much.

Tuesday 23rd January

The letter was ready for me to sign when I got into work. I cried as I was signing the letter. As I have some holiday accrued, I will be leaving as of now, which gives me more time to arrange things. All the girls were upset to see me leaving, as was

I, I love that job. The redundancy money I will transfer into my savings bank account. The books, cards and statements are in the red folder inside the suitcase, labelled 'bank'. There should be just shy of fifteen thousand pounds, enough to pay a housemaid/cleaner for a year or so.

Wednesday 24th January

The girls organised a lunch, a sort of a leaving party. It was such a sad experience, saying goodbye to them all, but at least I could say goodbye to them, in my way. They were all keen to know what I was going to do with my life. I could hardly say, 'well I only have a short life left to live,' so I said I had no idea. They gave me lots of suggestions; learn a new language, take up a new hobby or take a long holiday. The suggestions were great, I just smiled and thanked them for their concern and I will think about what to do now. Please apologise to them all for me. The lunch was fantastic and Laura baked one of her extraordinary cakes, with 'Sorry you are leaving' on it. I am not sure if it is possible, but maybe you could ask if they can have my wake at the library. Laura will enjoy baking cakes and I am sure all the other girls, will love being involved. Hopefully, the management will not disagree, as Nigel said, I am a valid member of staff.

Thursday 25th January

Grace phoned me; I have only been left one day. She was excited, telling me her plans for her fiftieth birthday in June. She is organising a cruise around the Mediterranean and was desperate for me to agree that I will go with her. She explained that even though it is a few months away, she wanted to get an accurate number, so she can pay the deposit and worry about the remainder of the money nearer the time. I said 'I would be delighted.' Please apologise to Grace for me and hopefully, she has not been left out of pocket. Wish her a wonderful fiftieth birthday for me. I have written her a card; can you give it to her on her birthday, please. There is only one envelope addressed to 'Grace' in the suitcase.

David found the birthday card, addressed to Grace. He thought about passing it to her now but didn't want to go against Joan's wishes and give it to her before her birthday.

Friday 26th January

Rattling around the house all day on my own, I decided to tidy a few cupboards. I found a pile of old photo albums, I sat looking through them and realised that once I am gone, you will have no idea who most of the people in them are. So, I removed some of the most important ones and wrote on the back, with the details of names, places and dates. Some of the dates may not be accurate, but they are as close as I could remember. I placed them in a pile on the table and they looked so sorry for themselves, just sitting in a pile, not being displayed, so I then went into to town and brought several photo albums and I have placed them in the albums, from earliest to latest. I am sure all the photo and albums have made the suitcase weigh an awful lot, which I apologise for. I hope they bring you some comfort in your darkest days.

David removed the photo albums from the suitcase. He decided to make himself a coffee and he sat back, looking through the photos and reading the reverse. Joan had written; date, place and who was in the photo, which David was thankful for, as he didn't know half of the people or the places in the pictures. He pulled out one of Joan and Adam as a baby and decided he would frame it, as she looked so happy and that is the memory he wished to keep.

Saturday 27th January

It was your niece Aimee's eighteenth birthday party in Devon. We had already planned to go and stay until Sunday. The party was a great event, it always is, if your brother arranges it. It was great to see all the family, although I felt a little upset that possibly the next time everyone will be together, will be at my funeral. At least I got to see everyone one more time, as some of them I haven't seen for years and most of them have kids of their own, that I have only seen photos of. You suggested that we should do something similar to Adam's sixteenth as an excuse for a family get together. I had to make my excuses at this moment, as it was too overwhelming and sat in the toilet, crying silently, as I didn't want to alert anyone to why I was upset.

David sat, staring into space, still clutching the diary. How will he find the strength to tell the family, the truth?

Sunday 28th January

When we got back from the amazing party, it was late afternoon. Adam went straight upstairs onto his computer, you had some work to do on your laptop and I sat on the sofa, watching trashy television and had little nap. Neither you nor Adam noticed me asleep, which was a relief, as having to explain why I was so exhausted, could have been difficult.

Chapter Eleven

Monday 29th January

Spending the weekend with your family and considering the next time everyone will be together will be at my funeral, I decided to start looking into arranging a funeral. I remember when my mother passed away and how much of a struggle it was arranging her funeral when all I wanted to do was hide under the duvet. I decided to contact the most local funeral directors to us, Smyth and Son's just off The High Street. I rang and spoke to a very friendly lady called Lorraine, she asked me to come down and meet with her. I once again caught the bus as I didn't want to have my car parked outside the funeral directors for anyone who knows us to start asking questions. Lorraine greeted me when I entered and immediately said 'I am so sorry for your loss.' I went a rather bright shade and didn't know how to answer. I realised that this is the reason I had not told anyone of my impending doom. I replied very sheepishly that I was arranging my funeral, which I expect will be within a couple of months. Poor Lorraine she looked so embarrassed. After she made me a cup of tea and we sat down, she talked me through the options of either a burial or a cremation, which I hadn't even considered before now. I settled on having a cremation, so I can then have my ashes scattered in our garden as I love the garden so much and Adam and you will have me close by to talk to. Lorraine also showed me a collection of coffins, some were very pricey and other moderately priced. I gave a lot of thought to this, you do only die once, but it seems such a waste of resources using all that wood and money for something I will be lying in for a few days, only then to be burnt to nothing but ashes. The coffin I have chosen is of moderate cost, but please if you do want to change it, I won't be offended, besides I won't even know as I will be dead! Lorraine asked me my thoughts on flowers and if I want everyone to send flowers or just close family. I hadn't thought about this either, but it makes sense that instead of flowers, friends should donate money to cancer research due to my illness. Flowers are lovely, you know how much I love flowers, but real money would be better spent trying to save the lives of others having to live with this hideous disease. I will ask that Adam and you choose a piece of music each to play at the funeral, I don't want to lay everything down in stone (excuse the pun), I do want you to be able to make some choices about the day. I have left Lorraine's business card in a white envelope with the name of Smyth and Sons funeral directors written on the front. Please give Lorraine a call, she is a lovely lady and she is fully prepared for the event and will take control of the whole process.

David dropped the diary on the floor and wept,

he was shocked and stunned to read what Joan
had gone through alone, arranging her funeral!
She was so brave to go through this illness alone
then arrange her funeral. What must her state of
mind have been in? 'She did all this and I never
even realised that she was ill.' David cried out.
David decided to shower and change his clothes
and visit Lorraine at the funeral directors.

Chapter Twelve

The sun was shining brightly following a heavy downpour of rain, Joan loved the April shower season, she always said that the heavy rain cleared the air and made everything in the garden grow. Tears started to fill his. David parked close to the funeral directors and before entering he reluctantly went into the newsagents next door to purchase ten cigarettes and he almost fainted when the shop assistant told him that cigarettes can only be brought in packets of twenty and then the cost. He hasn't smoked in over twenty years, but he felt as though he needed one right now. He stood outside the funeral directors inhaling the smoke deeply into his lungs, which was making him feel rather dizzy and wondered how anyone enjoyed this dirty habit. He was admiring the window display and thought how inviting it appeared, although once you are dead you don't go shopping for a funeral director, not everyone behaves like Joan did, arranging their funeral. He threw half the cigarette on the floor and stamped his foot on it, thinking he will never have another one. After he pushed the door when he heard a pleasant chime and a rather tall gentleman who was extremely smartly dressed in an expensive, three-piece suit and wearing a pocket watch in his waistcoat soon greeted him.

'Good day Sir, how can I help you?' The gentleman held out his hand.

'Hi, I am looking for a lady called Lorraine, she arranged my wife's funeral.' David held out his hand to shake his in return.

'Please take a seat, sir.' The Gentleman pointed to a comfy looking chair next to a table. "I will call Lorraine. Please can I get you a cup of tea or coffee?'

'I would appreciate a cup of coffee, white with two sugars please.' David sat down and started leafing through the literature that was left on the table. A short time later Lorraine arrived with a cup of coffee for David and a glass of water for herself.

'Good Morning David, I am Lorraine, I am pleased to meet you, I am sorry for your loss, Joan was a lovely lady. I understand that she didn't tell you she was ill did she?' Lorraine had a pained look on her face, whilst holding out her hand.

David wiped a tear from his face and attempted to speak but struggled to make a sound as he shook his head.

Lorraine gave a reassuring touch of David's hand. 'Take your time please David.'

David struggled to find the words. 'No, she didn't.

I am amazed that she went through all this hurt alone.'

David gave a limp shake of Lorraine's hand.

'She was a very brave lady.' Lorraine took a sip of her water.

'I understand that she has arranged everything before she died and I do not need to arrange anything?'

Lorraine put her hand on David's again to comfort him. 'You do still need to arrange the date and time and location, but yes, she has arranged and paid for everything. There are still other details we can discuss.

Do you have a date in mind?'

'I hadn't thought about it, how long do people usually leave it after death until the funeral?'

'It depends, each situation is different, but we could provisionally book something for Friday the twenty-fourth. Do you have any relatives or friends that need to travel from a distance?'

'I think so, why?'

Lorraine thumbed through her diary. 'It would be best to book a later time in the day, giving other's time to arrive for the funeral service. If you have it too early, then some people may not be able to attend.'

'Yes, that is a good thought. Can I suggest two o'clock?' David was feeling very queasy and not enjoying the experience at all.

'I will schedule for two o'clock. I will leave you to think about which venue you wish to use. Joan did suggest a crematorium, do you have any preference to which one?'

David started looking very pale and felt as though he was about to faint.

Lorraine could see this. 'David, you are not looking very well, can I suggest that you get some rest as you have had a lot to deal with and we can talk about this tomorrow, there is plenty of time.' Lorraine gave David a reassuring touch of the arm.

'Thank you, it has all been a little overwhelming, to say the least. I will call in and see you tomorrow sometime.' David stood up and almost fell over the table they were sat at.

Lorraine was startled. 'Please, David sit back down and finish your coffee, there is no rush, take your time to get your strength back before you drive home.'

'Thank you.' David sat back down again and felt rather foolish for almost falling over, but Lorraine was right, he shouldn't drive home right now feeling as queasy as he did.

David woke up and realised that he had fallen asleep in the comfy chair in the funeral director's office.

'Hi David, how are you feeling?' Lorraine greeted him with a friendly smile.

'Oh my gosh, I am so sorry, how embarrassing falling asleep in your office.' He looked at his watch and realised he had been there for almost two hours. David tried to rise quickly again, but he's legs gave way and he fell back down.

'David please, you do not need to apologise, I need to check that you are okay before you leave, this is a very trying time.' Lorraine asked her colleague to get David a cup of coffee. 'We are here to support the bereaved also you know, we're not just a dispatching service.'

David managed a smile. 'Thank you, I appreciate it. It's so hard dealing with this all alone.'

'Do you not have any family who can help you with the arrangements?'

'My son is only twelve years old and is being looked after by Joan's Sister currently.'

Lorraine handed David a fresh cup of coffee.

'Please take your time. I have booked the closest crematorium provisionally whilst you have been sleeping, so, if that is okay, you can at least start informing people and inviting them. But please don't feel pressurized, as there is still plenty of time.'

David sipped his coffee, which was delightfully hot. 'That sounds great, I will start inviting people, maybe I can put an obituary in the local press and also, a notice in the library where she worked for many years, I am sure all the regulars would be interested to know of the details.'

'That is a lovely idea, I can prepare something for you to take to the press and the library.' Lorraine was at her desk and tapping away on her computer keyboard before David had a chance to say thank you.

David finished his coffee and thanked Lorraine. Lorraine handed David two pieces of paper, with details Joan's funeral, for the; press and the library. 'Thank you for your help and once again I am sorry for falling asleep.' David held out his hand.

Lorraine shook David's hand. 'If you have any questions, please do not hesitate to call me.

Everything is booked for two o clock on the twenty-fourth.'

David turned and left the funeral directors and the first thing he did once he got outside was light another cigarette.

Chapter Thirteen

Tuesday 30th January

I have received a few more applications for the housemaid job. A few of them are more suitable than the first few. I have made a shortlist, of those that I would like to interview. The jobcentre and I agreed, we will keep the vacancy open for three weeks, so maybe some more will come in before I have to arrange an interview.

Wednesday 31st January

I felt exhausted today. So, I did nothing, just sat in front of the television, watching daytime programmes. I am amazed that so many of the programmes that were on, when I was home on maternity leave are still showing. They are popular.

Thursday 1st February

I met the girls from work for lunch. They want to make it a regular event, at least once a month. Which I was delighted with. They are all missing

Friday 2nd February

David felt guilty that he spent so much time on his laptop, not paying much attention to Joan. If only she had told him, he would have put his laptop down and spent more time with her.

Saturday 3rd February

You were keen for us to go back to the D.I.Y store, as you needed a couple of items to finish the painting of the living room. I convinced you that if you went alone, it would be quicker. I couldn't face another visit to that store, where you look at other items and suggest that we decorate other rooms. It will not be important to me, once I am gone.

Saturday 3rd February

I have received several more emails from prospective workers regarding the advert in the jobcentre, most of which asked the same question 'When would you want someone to start?' I explained that it would not be until a few months, but there is no definite date as yet. This is something I am going to have to come to terms with, I can only imagine what life would have been like if I had told everyone I was dying, they would be questioning me all the time. I have arranged a few interviews for the twenty-first of February and I have given them each an hour of my time. I have no idea if that is the right amount of time, but the lady in the jobcentre said it would be a good choice as one candidate may arrive late and another early. Five prospective candidates all lined up for an interview an hour apart. Gosh, I am going to be tired when I have *finished. Just enough time to see them whilst Adam is at school and you are at work, so neither of you will know. I have decided not to tell the candidates of my impending doom, just that our lives are going to get busy in a few months and that is when the job will start from. It may put some people off, knowing their prospective boss has to die first, before they start work.*

David walked into the kitchen and flicked the switch down on the kettle to make a cup of coffee. As he stood waiting for the kettle to boil, he started perusing the many pieces of paper stuck to the fridge with an assortment of magnets. Mostly they were relevant to Adam; school plays, parents evening, football practice and school trips. The one about the trip to The Science Museum in London caught his eye, as the date was February the twenty-first. 'How clever.' He mumbled to himself. The kettle clicked off and David filled his cup with hot water and stirred the coffee thoroughly whilst adding two sugars. Joan used to moan about him having two sugars in his coffee. She was always telling him that it can cause lots of health problems and that he could die a young man. Where was the irony in that, Joan never ate processed foods, exercised and she was the one dead at forty-one years of age? David returned to the living room, turned on the television and sat back with Joan's diary in his hand to read on.

Sunday 4th February

The living room looks lovely now it has been finished. Well done, I am proud of you. It must be nice to do something other than working all the time. I am sorry, I won't be able to appreciate all your hard work for much longer.

Monday 5th February

I have had a few more applications for the housemaid vacancy I advertised. My shortlist will take me a week to interview them all, so I have had to shortlist, my shortlist.

Tuesday 6th February

There has been one final application arrive today. I think she may be the one, but I am reserving my judgement until I have met with her and the others I have shortlisted.

Wednesday 7th February

I arranged the interviews, I had to shortlist my short-listed shortlist. Otherwise, I would be interviewing for days on end. I have four people coming along, with time to space them out during the day, as the lady in the jobcentre suggested.

Thursday 8th February

I spent the day, sorting out paperwork; health insurance, all the paperwork for my car and anything else you may need. It has all been placed in the envelope titled 'paperwork.'

Friday 9th February

I spent the day sorting more drawers and cupboards out. I came across, so many pieces of paper with names and addresses for friends and relatives. I decided to go into town and purchase a new address book. The tatty one I found, had so many names and addresses scrubbed out, which is what I do, when they have moved house or, are no longer with us. I am sure that most of the friends and relatives, will not be able to attend my funeral, but at least you can let them know.

David found the new address book, with names and addresses of friends and family, neatly written out. At least he now had a list of people he needed to make contact with.

Saturday 10th February

It was a pleasant winters day, the sun shining brightly, but bitterly cold. You took Adam and me to a pub for lunch, it was situated along the canal, one that I have never eaten in before. I am sure I never will visit there again, but I enjoyed the food. We took a walk along the canal afterwards, to walk off the large lunch. It was lovely to spend some quality time together as a family, not rushing, not working, just enjoying the outside and our company.

Sunday 11th February

Adam was at a friend's house and you were busy working on your laptop. I spent most of the day, lazing in front of the television, watching box sets. Once I had finished a series, I realised, I won't see the next series.

Monday 12th February

Lorraine from the funeral directors rang me, she was just asking a few more questions to finalise a few arrangements. She is a lovely lady, please do thank her again.

Tuesday 13th February

I met the girls from work for lunch again. I was trying to think of an excuse to cancel, as I couldn't face anymore questioning, regarding what my plans are. I decided that as the lunch date was for my benefit, it would be rude of me to cancel. It was great to see the girls again. I do miss them all. They are missing me equally as much. They did ask questions regarding my plans, I told them I was looking at an evening class, learning a new hobby, which doesn't start until September.

Wednesday 14th February

You came home from work, with a huge bouquet and a card, with flight tickets inside, taking us to Paris. I have always wanted to go to Paris, thank you for this. I just wished it could have been a different time, when I may not enjoy it. I felt awful, that with everything going on, I had forgotten it was Valentines weekend. You had even arranged for Adam to spend the weekend at my sisters.

David remembered Joan's reaction to the trip. She was pleased, but now he thinks back to that day, there was a slight hesitation in her reaction, one that he wouldn't have expected, but he didn't think anything of it. He just thought she must have had a bad day at work.

Thursday 15th February

I had an appointment with our lovely Doctor. She talked through the pain management options. I said I didn't want to take anything at present as it will be more useful to take it when I need it.

Friday 16th February

I spent the day watching daytime television, trying to conserve my energy, for the hectic weekend ahead.

Saturday 17th February

We got up at four am and left for the airport, for the short flight to Paris. I was delighted to visit one of the most romantic cities in the world, I just wished I had more energy to be able to enjoy it all. You wanted to see as many of the sights as possible and so did I. I was exhausted, but I didn't let on and kept up with your enthusiasm and had a wonderful time. I did want to go back to the hotel earlier than you wanted to, but I tried to cover my exhaustion with an excuse, I had a cold coming. I am so eternally grateful for the effort you went to, to organise the weekend, I can honestly say the last weekend we spent together was in the most idyllic city.

David remembered how unwell Joan looked and that she said she had a cold coming. Why couldn't she have told him the truth, he wouldn't have taken her around so many museums and beauty spots and let her take more rests.

Sunday 18th February

Thankfully, you had arranged a less hectic day. Taking me on a boat ride down the river Seine and having lunch on board the boat. It was an amazing weekend, but I was glad to board the flight home. Adam was back home, as my sister had kindly driven him home. I decided to unpack tomorrow as I was exhausted, saying my cold was definitely on its way.

Monday 19th February

The girls from work wanted to meet for lunch. They wanted to hear all about my trip to Paris at the weekend. They bombarded me with questions; did I enjoy it? What was the best bit? Would I ever go back? I had to tell a lie to the last question, saying I would love to go back one day.

Tuesday 20th February

I plan to interview the candidates for the housemaid vacancy tomorrow. So, me being me, I tidied the house, so it didn't look a mess to the interviewees.

David looked around the house and failed to see how the house was ever in a mess. Joan did think the house was in a mess, if one shoe was out of place on the shoe rack, or one curtain didn't hang right.

Chapter Fourteen

Wednesday 21st February

Well David I interviewed the candidates today. I am glad I never did that as a full-time occupation, it was so stressful and tiring. Just as the lady in The Job Centre had speculated the timings were adequate. The first candidate arrived thirty minutes late and the second one fifteen minutes early. I won't bore you with the entire day, just that three, were so unsuitable, I wouldn't even let them look after our dog (if we had one that is!) Elizabeth was the favourite for me. She was such a gentle young lady from Eastern Europe somewhere. She spoke great English and her manners were impeccable. I explained that the vacancy would not be available for a few months yet, which she accepted. I explained that my husband David would give her a call when she is required to start work. She asked where I was going? I explained that I am planning to go out of the country for a while. What else could I say without saying too much? Please say hello to Elizabeth and apologise to her for lying, but I couldn't tell anyone of my plans. You will find the details for Elizabeth in a white envelope with Elizabeth written on the front. Give her a call and tell her that you are Joan's wife David and she is required to start working as soon as she is free.

David rummaged in the suitcase and there was a white envelope with the name Elizabeth written on it. Inside was a piece of paper with an address and mobile telephone number scribbled in Joan's handwriting. He held the paper for some time before he plucked up the courage to dial the number.

'Hello, Elizabeth speaking.' A young lady answered.

'Hi Elizabeth, it is David, Joan's husband.' David struggled to get the words out of his mouth.

'Ah David, yes Joan said you will be calling me.

How is she please?'

'Umm, this is not a very good line, could you come to my house and I will explain?' David was struggling to hold back the tears.

'Of course, yes. Is now convenient for you, I am just in the town centre, I can be with you in around an hour if that is okay?' Elizabeth was shouting over the noise of a shop's choice of music if you could call the racquet, they were playing music.

'That will be lovely Elizabeth, come when you are ready, please there is no rush.' David ended the call on his mobile and cried once again.

Whilst David was flicking through the television channels a ring of the doorbell startled him. He slowly rose and shuffled to the door to open it and found standing there on the doorstep was a very stunning, blond, twenty-something girl smiling sweetly and holding out her hand. 'You must be David, yes?' She spoke whilst smiling.

'Yes, I am, please do come in.' David opened the door and gestured for her to come inside, trying to hide his tears.

'How is Joan, she said she has to go away and that is why you need a housemaid?'

'Elizabeth, I have some bad news, please sit down.' David signalled to the sofa. 'Joan died a few days ago. I have only just found out that she interviewed you and asked you to come and work for me. She planned her final days on this earth, she knew she was dying and she also knew that I would be stuck unable to keep the house clean and tidy.' David saw the tears well up in Elizabeth's eyes. David sat beside her and hugged her tightly and they cried together until Elizabeth broke the silence.

'Why did she not tell anyone? She told you though, yes?' Elizabeth showed pain on her face.

'Sadly no, she didn't. She left a diary and a series of instructions in there telling me what she has been doing and who to contact. I have no idea what else I am likely to find.' David sobbed.

'I am so sorry David; Joan was such a kind caring, lady. I have no words that can heal your pain I am sure. All I can say is that I am ready to start work for you as soon as you need me.' Elizabeth wiped the tears from her eye's trying not to smudge her make up.

'Thank you, Elizabeth, anytime tomorrow would be marvelous, I would be grateful of some company to be fair.' David pleaded.

'Of course, David, I will be here at ten o'clock. Do you need me to bring anything? Have you eaten? You don't look like you have eaten?' Elizabeth enquired.

'No, I haven't eaten very much, just a microwave meal and I overcooked that, I am not in the mood to cook at the moment.' David admitted.

'No problem David, I will bring some homemade soup with me, if you don't like it, I won't mind.' Elizabeth made a note in her phone of a list of ingredients to buy on the way home to make the soup. 'I will leave you and let you get on and I will see you tomorrow morning. I know it is hard, but please try and get some rest.' Elizabeth held out her hand to shake David's and made her way towards the front door. David was feeling tired again so decided to get himself in bed and read some more of Joan's diary.

Thursday 22nd February

I went into town and printed the photos from the weekend, that I took on my phone. I have placed them in a photo album, it is smaller than the one that contains all the other photos from all the years together.

David found the photo album, there were several photos from their weekend. Joan had also included the flight tickets and the hotel's business card. Such a lovely memory from the weekend.

Friday 23rd February

I had a couple of emails asking if I had decided on the position yet? I realised that I had to let the other candidates know that I have made a decision. I cannot believe how desperate people are for a part-time job. I am too tired today, maybe I will tackle the task tomorrow.

Saturday 24th February

I emailed the unsuccessful candidates. Only one replied and asked why? I didn't want to get into a long email correspondence, so I just replied saying I was unable to give feedback.

Sunday 25th February

I decided to have a day, sat watching daytime television. I am quite enjoying watching all the same programmes I watched when I was on maternity leave. It brings back memories of when Adam was a baby. I am still shocked that he has grown into a fine young man already.

Monday 26th February

Adam was off school poorly. I took him to the Doctors, thankfully, the Doctor didn't ask how I was feeling, otherwise, that would have been awkward. Next time you see the Doctor, can you thank her for me, for being so discreet. Adam slept most of the day, so was unaware of me laying around on the sofa.

Tuesday 27th February

Adam was still at home from school. You offered to stay off with him instead of me, but I convinced you that I don't mind staying home. You felt it was unfair as I was off yesterday, but after some persuasion, I managed to convince you, Adam would rather his mum, look after him. I couldn't pretend to go to work and stay out all day, that would have been deceitful of me, but then I suppose, I have been deceitful through all of this. I am sorry.

Wednesday 28th February

I invited Elizabeth over for a coffee and a chat, just to go through things with her. She is popping over tomorrow.

Thursday 1st March

Elizabeth arrived promptly at ten o clock as she said she would. She is a lovely girl and I have every confidence in her that she will keep the house looking lovely and that nothing will be too much trouble for her.

Friday 2nd March

You were working from home and questioned why I wasn't at work. I told you I had some leave to use up. It wasn't a lie; I was using up my leave

Saturday 3rd March

Your annual work event, which normally I look forward to. It's one of the few times in the year I get a chance to dress up and spend the weekend in a luxury hotel. Only this year was more stressful than fun. If I could have got out of going I would, but I didn't want to alert you to why I didn't want to go. The dinner was amazing as always, although I am slowly losing my appetite each day, which was such a shame as the food was delicious. It was great to see all your work colleagues, apart from the constant questioning, 'where and when are we going on holiday?' Adam enjoyed the entertainment and catching up with all the other kids.

David felt guilty that he had tired Joan out so much. If he knew of her illness, he would have made other arrangements for the weekend, such as going alone or not staying over and leaving the party earlier.

Sunday 4th March

We went for a walk in the grounds of the hotel, which was lovely; cold and crisp morning, with the low bright sun shining. Adam collected some cones for a school project. We stopped on the way home, for a pub lunch.

Monday 5th March

All I could manage today was sleep. I had such a lovely weekend, but it was exhausting.

Chapter Fifteen

Tuesday 6th March

One of them charities knocked today. Asking if I can make regular payments to a children's cancer charity. I cannot imagine, children suffering from this awful disease. I invited the young chap in and made him a cup of tea, he was frozen to the bone, from the pouring rain. The young chap; Matt and I had a lovely chat. He explained to me, why he chooses to do the work he does. He lost his sister when she was four years old and he was only six years old himself. This is such a cruel world, why does cancer, take children away. I would very much like you to continue to support the charity, once I have passed. It is only a few pounds a month, the charity does such great things for the children that are suffering and their family. Matt explained, that when his sister was ill, his family had no support and he wishes they did. I have added the details of the charity into an envelope, marked 'Children's Charity'. In there is my confirmation of my donation agreement.

David found the envelope, in the suitcase and read the amount of money that Joan was donating each month. She was such a generous soul.

Wednesday 7th March

I have been busy preparing tonight's dinner, which is Adam and your favourite, lasagne. This gave me a thought that if the feeding of you two after I am gone were left to you, it would be take-a-ways and microwave meals every day of the week. I then spent the day collating all of the recipes that I cook regularly. In the yellow folder, there is a compilation of recipes, some of your favourite; lasagne, hot pot, roast dinner (including how to make the perfect Yorkshire puddings) and chilli con Carne. Also, I have included some of your favourite puddings; steamed pudding, chocolate cake and crumble. On compiling this list, I realised that you won't be able to understand the terminology listed in the recipes so I have made a list of the most common terms used in cooking.

• Baste: This is when you pour fat over the food, when roasting chicken or turkey, you baste the food in cooking oil.

• Blanch: This is when you boil a pan of water and then throw the food in for a few minutes and then into ice-cold water, such as vegetables.

• Beat: You do this when making batter or whisking eggs, using a fork and stir vigorously.

• Blind bake: If you make a pastry base that you need to cook before you fill it, you add greaseproof paper and then place some dried beans on top to keep the shape of the pastry whilst baking.

• Cream: When making cakes you rub the butter with the sugar against the side of the bowl with the back of a spoon.

• Fold: This is when you add egg whites to a mixture, you place the lighter ingredients on top of the heavier mixture and fold the ingredients together until they are mixed.

• Knead: If you make bread you have to push down and away from you on the dough, it becomes shiny and smooth.

• Rub, when a recipe says to rub, it means that you pick the ingredients up in your fingers and rub the butter and flour together between your fingertips. The ingredients will look like breadcrumbs when you have finished rubbing them together.

I have collated all the recipes in a grey folder. Please try and cook proper meals for Adam and yourself, I wouldn't want him living on take-a-way or microwave meals. Maybe book yourself onto a cookery course, it will do you the world of good. Enjoy looking through the folder and sorry that some of the recipes are slightly weathered from many years of use, as you will see.

David thumbed through the pile of recipes in the grey folder. Some were torn; some were covered in food and others were soiled in various liquids. He looked in amazement at the number of recipes that were there, he knew that Joan cut them out religiously and it always amazed him why she did it, he questioned her every time she did, however, he was thankful at this moment in time that she had. Then at the bottom of the pile of torn out recipes was an envelope in which Joan had written on the front.

'Please enjoy learning to cook. I have booked a cookery course for you. XXX.'

Inside the envelope was a gift voucher for the local cookery school for a one day 'Learning the basics about cookery course'. The voucher had an expiry of the seventh of March, next year and all he needed to do was to call the school to book the cookery course on a day that was convenient to him.

Chapter Sixteen

Thursday 8th March

I did some food shopping today. It was a struggle, just carrying a few bags from the car to the house. I think I am going to start using an online delivery service from now on.

Friday 9th March

I went shopping to buy a wedding gift, for your friends, daughter who is getting married tomorrow. Thankfully it didn't take me long to find the perfect gift. As I don't think I could have coped with trailing around more shops than I had to.

Saturday 10th March

We travelled to London, for the wedding of your friend's daughter. We were put up in a lovely hotel, along with the rest of the wedding party, paid for by your friend. I don't think there were any other guests other than the several hundred wedding guests, staying in the hotel. It was a beautiful ceremony. The wedding breakfast was exquisite. Rebecca and Joshua were amazingly happy and so pleased that so many guests shared their special day. The entertainment was amazing and we didn't retire to our magnificent bedroom until after midnight.

Sunday 11th March

Thankfully the hotel, served breakfast until eleven o clock as we didn't wake until just after ten o clock. We chatted to lots of your friends that you haven't seen for years and you insisted that they must come and visit us in the summer. I just nodded and said it will be lovely to see them.

Monday 12th March

I visited the doctor today. We chatted about my pain management, as I am feeling I need something stronger. She still didn't pressure me to tell you and Adam, she respects my decision. I wonder if any other of her patients have done the same?

Tuesday 13th March

The medication is certainly helping with the pain, but the side effect is that it is making me very sleepy. I decided not to fight the sleep and spent the day, lying on the sofa, watching daytime television.

Wednesday 14th March

I was completely shocked today. An old school friend looked me up on Facebook. She is friends with someone I am friends with and that is how she found me. Sarah, that's her name, was so excited when she messaged me, she said she has been looking for me for years. She wants to meet for lunch one day next week. I feel terrible that she has finally found me and I won't be around for much longer.

Thursday 15th March

I contacted a local solicitor today. I need to look at writing a will. Not that I have much to leave, but I think it's the sensible thing to do. I remember some of my friends and the struggles they had when a family member passed without making a will.

Friday 16th March

The postman delivered one of my loyalty card reward vouchers. This got me thinking that I need to collate them all, so you can get them transferred into your name. Some of them have several pounds on them, it may not be much, but it all adds up. In the envelope, marked 'Loyalty cards', you will find all of the cards. I can't believe how many I have, no wonder I couldn't close my purse fully.

Saturday 17th March

I managed to get Adam out on his bike, all he does is sit in front of his computer, but then he must take after you. Please do try and get Adam to take more exercise.

Sunday 18th March

I could only manage, lying on the sofa watching awful television, but reading a novel, that I will finish.

Monday 19th March

I started thinking about what to put in my will and making a list, so when I see the solicitor I will be prepared. I did get quite emotional doing it.

Tuesday 20th March

I met Sarah for lunch. Gosh, she hasn't changed a bit, but then neither have I, according to her. We were thick as thieves at school. We shared some memories; good ones and also some memories I would rather forget. We did laugh though. I needed the laugh. She is keen to meet up once a month. I agreed, what else could I say. Her name and contact details are in the address book, 'Sarah Williams.' Please apologise to her for me.

David thumbed through the address book and phoned the details for Sarah. He was going to put off calling her until another day but thought he had better do it sooner.

Wednesday 21st March

I started tidying cupboards up today. I couldn't imagine you having to go through all my things, so I made a start for you. Putting items in boxes and bags.

Thursday 22nd March

I went through my wardrobe and put clothes, shoes and handbags in bags and boxes, so you don't have to clear them out yourself.

Friday 23rd March

I decided that there are too many boxes and bags of my things, stacked up in cupboards. So, I took them to the local charity shop, 'Cancer Research.' I felt that the choice of the shop was appropriate. The assistant asked had I lost someone recently as I had so many boxes and bags. I just nodded.

David put the diaries down and decided to phone Sarah. The phone only rang a couple of rings, before a cheery voice answered.

'Hello, can I help you?' Sarah spoke.

David didn't know how to reply and struggled for a moment.

'Hello, is there anyone there?' Sarah asked.

'Sorry,' David started, 'I am David, the wife of your old school friend Joan.'

Sarah sounded delighted to hear from him. 'How are you, Joan has told me so many lovely things about you....'

David interrupted, 'Can you come over to the house? I have something I need to discuss with you.'

There was silence from Sarah before she asked, 'What is it? Is Joan okay?'

David didn't want to tell Sarah over the phone. 'Please can you come over? I will speak to you in more detail then.'

Sarah realised the urgency of David's call. 'Of course, it will take me about thirty minutes to get to you.'

David nodded his head and realised; Sarah couldn't see him. 'Thanks.' He muttered and then ended the call.

Chapter Seventeen

Sarah arrived as she had promised within thirty minutes. The look on David's face when he opened the front door, told Sarah all she needed to know, without David muttering a word.

'It is bad news, isn't it?' Sarah quizzed.

David nodded. He invited Sarah to sit and explained everything to her. Sarah was crying so much; he didn't know if he should offer a cuddle to comfort her. He decided to hand her a box of tissues instead. Sarah was struggling to take the news in. Having only just found her after losing touch with her for many years, since school. David made them both a cup of coffee and they drank in silence, not knowing what to say to one another. After a while, she said she had somewhere to be. David didn't press her any further as he realised the real reason she was leaving; was she was too upset to stay.

David struggled to understand why Joan agreed to meet up with an old school friend and subject her to all the sorrow that she was now experiencing. Maybe she was curious to see her one more time before she passed.

Chapter Eighteen

David started to regret the decision to buy the cigarette's as he was beginning to feel hooked again. He drove his car to the library and found a parking space directly outside. He lit another cigarette whilst plucking up the courage to enter and speak to Joan's colleagues. The automatic door opened and immediately Grace saw David enter. 'Hello David, it's lovely to see you. How is Joan doing? We haven't seen her in here for a while, we were only saying this morning we haven't seen her for ages, didn't we Linda.' Grace nudged Linda in the ribs. David was stunned by Grace's enthusiasm to see him, she had no idea that she had passed, or was indeed ill. He plucked up the courage to speak.

'Grace is there somewhere we can go that is quiet?'

Grace laughed. 'This is a library David, everywhere is quiet.'

'Sorry, I mean somewhere private?' David quizzed.

'You are frightening me, David, what is it, is Joan OK?' Grace's face turned from happy to concerned.

'Please Grace, can we go somewhere....'

'Come into the office.' Grace interrupted and led the way. 'Please is Joan okay, what is it?'

Once they had both sat down, David started to explain. 'I am sorry Grace, but Joan passed away a few days ago.' David was struggling to hold back the tears.

Grace gasped whilst holding her hands over her mouth as she tried to speak. 'Oh my god, how, why?'

'She had been ill for several months and didn't want anyone to know she was dying.' David tried to put on a brave face.

'Oh my god, that is awful for you both, what have you two been going through the last few months?' Grace leant forward with her head in her hands, to shield her tears.

'That is another thing Grace, she never told anyone, not even me. She left a series of letters and diaries telling me what she has been up to the past few months, I cannot believe she struggled through the illness alone.'

'On my gosh, she didn't even tell you?' Tears started streaming from her eyes.

'That's right, she didn't want to upset me. Good old Joan, she always did think of everyone else before herself.'

'How is Adam? Oh my god, poor Adam, he must be so confused.'

'Adam is with Joan's sister, Eleanor, I didn't want him to be subjected to me having to arrange a funeral and everything and then I found the diaries.' David was staring into space.

'Oh my gosh, if there is anything, I can do for you, please do let me know, it cannot be easy going through this alone.' Grace placed her hand over his.

'Thank you I appreciate that. I have the details of the funeral here.' David handed Grace the paper that Lorraine had prepared. 'I was wondering if you could let the regular customers and Joan's colleagues know, I am sure she would be delighted if any of them can make it.'

'Of course, we will shut the library for the afternoon.' Grace informed him whilst reading the details she had just been given.

'Thank you, Joan asked if we could hold the wake here? She spent so much time in here, she felt it would be the most fitting place.'

'Of course, we can. I will speak to Nigel; I am sure he will not object.'

'Thank you, can I leave you to let all the other colleagues know, I don't think I can face anyone else today, I will fill you in on the details of the diaries some other time, I am feeling rather tired now.' David got up to leave.

'Of course, please take care of yourself and I will see you at the funeral, but please give me a call if you need anything.' Grace rummaged for a scrap of paper and scribbled her number hastily on the paper and handed it to David.

'Thank you.' David took the piece of paper, folded it in half and placed it in his trouser pocket. He turned to leave, not looking at anyone as he left the library, so he did not have to face anyone and for them to see the tears streaming down his face.

Chapter Nineteen

David arrived home after visiting the library and ordered himself a take-a-way pizza. He sat back and read some more. Realising how far he had reached so far, there couldn't be much more to read.

Saturday 24th March

I spent most of the day, cooking food and freezing it. You didn't notice as you were working, as usual. At least there are a few meals in the freezer for you to eat for a few days.

Sunday 25th March

The weather was rather nice, for March, anyway. I spent most of the day in the garden. I love the garden, please do remember to scatter my ashes in the garden, I can always be there then.

Monday 26th March

I had an appointment with the solicitor. We talked through the will and he said he will have it drawn up in a day or two and I will need to go back and sign it.

Tuesday 27th March

After the meeting with the solicitor to finalise my will, I felt really low today. It just seems final now.

Wednesday 28th March

I met the girls from work for lunch. I was very quiet, but they were so wrapped up in their own drama's they didn't notice, thankfully. I don't know how I would have explained my somber mood.

Thursday 29th March

I went back to the solicitor to sign my will. It is inside an envelope 'last will and testament'. The details of the solicitors are written within the will. Please thank the solicitor for me, for being so prompt and considerate to my wish to keep my illness a secret.

Friday 30th March

I went back to the doctors today. We chatted

*through my options. I will probably have to go into
a hospice soon. I am feeling very tired, in lots of
pain and not coping very well.*

Saturday 31st March

*Thankfully, you were busy working and Adam
was at a friend's that you didn't notice how tired I
was.*

Sunday 1st April

*Thankfully, you were busy working and Adam
was on his computer that neither of you didn't
notice how tired I was.*

Monday 2nd April

*I visited the doctors again. She has given me
an increase in pain medication.*

Tuesday 3rd April

*I slept most of the day. I think the fateful day of
needing to tell you, is coming very soon.*

Wednesday 4th April

All I have to say is, I am sorry, for not telling you. Once the time went on, it got harder. Hopefully, all the organising I have done will make things easier for you.

Chapter Twenty

Thursday 5th April

Dear David, I think this may be my last diary entry. I am feeling very poorly and exhausted all the time. Today I had the Doctor come and visit me at home as I was too poorly to even go out. The Doctor said that I should think about going into a hospice, she understands my decision not to tell my family and she respects my wish, she said I am a very brave lady. I had to agree with her that a hospice is a good idea as I do feel that fateful day will be upon me very soon. She said she would make some enquiries and give me a call later. I thanked her immensely. True to her word, the Doctor called me later in the afternoon and said that the local hospice has space for me to go and stay. She did say that I have to now tell you as the end is nigh and you will have to drive me there! This is not something I am looking forward to, but it has to be done. I am too ill to cook dinner tonight, so I am planning to order a take-a-way. I know I hate take-a-way food, full of all those chemicals, but it is not going to kill me is it? This cancer is doing a fine job of that on its own! Please be assured I tried to tell you on so many occasions, but I could not bring myself to be the bearer of such bad news. I will always love you and I am truly thankful for our time together. Please give Adam lots of hugs and kisses from me and please, please never tell him about this, I would not like him to think I have betrayed him. I think too much of him and I only wanted to protect him.

XXXXXXXXXXXXXXX

David remembered the conversation that evening. Joan said she had ordered a take-a-way, which David was truly stunned at her actions. She said she had something to tell him that was important and needed to have his undivided attention. His first thought was that she had found someone else and she was leaving him. He didn't think for one minute that she was dying. He cried in her arms, so much that he soaked her favourite top with his tears. She reassured him that she was going to be fine and that the cancer is aggressive and that she doesn't have much time left, but wants to go into a hospice as it will be peaceful and she will be supported by lots of nurses who will be able to assist in looking after her. Joan didn't want to burden David with the job of looking after her until the end of her days when there is a perfectly good hospice down the road. She suggested that he visited and stayed as often as he could. David had realised that she was tired more often, but had no idea it was because she was dying. After dinner Joan went to their bedroom and packed a few things as if she were going on holiday, not to die! David found this all a little overwhelming how a woman who has been told she doesn't have long left is taking everything in her stride. Since reading her diaries he knows how she coped so well, as she had been ready for the last day of her life for several months. He remembered her saying goodbye to Adam and that she would be back soon, she was just going away to have a little rest, as she was tired. Adam cried his heart out and I think he knew more than he let on to Joan. 'You will have fun at Eleanor's, you know she always spoils you.'

Joan tried to calm him with her words. David drove to Eleanor's first, as she agreed to have Adam stay for a few days.

The hospice was such a picturesque building set in acres and acres of beautiful grounds. A nurse appeared from the main entrance with a wheelchair to take Joan to her room, which was very light and airy, just the way she liked it. David helped Joan get into her nightdress and settled her into bed and then went to the kitchen and made her a cup of tea. On the way to the kitchen, a nurse pulled David to one side and asked how he was feeling. David wasn't sure how he was feeling as everything had happened so fast.

On returning from the kitchen with a cup of tea for Joan, a lady was in Joan's room talking to her and she introduced herself as Sandra the social worker and said that she was there for both of them and that if he ever needed to talk then all he had to do was knock on her door. David was too frightened to leave Joan that night and made arrangements for Eleanor to have Adam stay overnight with her so he could stay the night at the hospice. He slept in the chair that did recline very slightly, it was such an uncomfortable sleep, but he couldn't rest easy as he was keeping an eye on Joan and assisting her if she needed the toilet or a drink as she was struggling to move alone. The nurses were coming in and out all-night checking that she was comfortable and changing her morphine pump. David was always led to believe, the end was close when a patient was on morphine, but at this time, he hoped it was just a myth. This same routine went on for several days until one day Joan who was looking a lot perkier asked if Adam could come and visit, as she wanted to say her goodbyes. David wept and couldn't begin to imagine how he was going to tell Adam that his mother was in a hospice and she was dying, but later that day Eleanor, brought Adam to see her.   Adam looked so scared entering the vast building and seeing his mum in bed hooked up to medical tubes and this just made him all the more anxious. David had no idea what was said between them as he left them alone and went and made another cup of tea for Joan and a coffee for himself. Adam was crying and hugging his mum so much when he returned and Adam asked if he could go home. He kissed his mum on the forehead and said his goodbye's, that was the last time they saw each other, but at least, Adam saw her in a good way and he can remember her in good spirits, not as she was in the final days when her body shut down and she was just lying there unable to move or even speak until all the life was taken from her and she was no more. Elanor also spent some time with Joan and that was the last time they saw each other.

Chapter Twenty-one

Friday 27th April

David was anxiously waiting for the funeral cars to. Everyone was talking quietly so they did not disturb David's thoughts. Adam was being comforted by his Auntie Eleanor and looked so smart in his black suit; his mother would have been proud of him.

The funeral cars arrived on time at one thirty as the funeral directors had promised and all the family made their way to the cars. Adam sat huddled against David in the car ride to the crematorium, he was crying like a baby. David was struggling not to cry but thought there is probably plenty of time left for that before the end of the day.

The twenty-minute journey felt like two hours, being driven along at ten miles per hour with so many people stopping and standing to attention as they rolled past. When they finally reached the crematorium, David was gob smacked by the number of mourners there, at least one hundred if not more. Friends, family, customers, colleagues, some people that he had not seen for many, many years. The press obituary and the information in the library had helped. After they emerged from the car, so many people greeted Adam and David, they all gave their condolences with hugs and kisses and many of them he did not even know, but he thanked them for coming along all the same. David helped carry Joan's coffin into the crematorium, which he wondered how he would have the strength to do so right now and was so paranoid he was going to drop it and her body was going to fall out and roll across the floor, but he managed to find the strength from somewhere. The service was beautiful and he could not have asked for a better send-off.

After the service they all went back to the library where Grace and Linda had arranged the wake, they had organised all the food as promised and closed the library for the afternoon, not that is mattered as most of the regular library customers were at the service.

Lorraine, from the funeral directors, approached David and handed him a letter. 'This is from Joan, she asked me to hand it to you after the funeral.' David stared at the letter before taking it from Lorraine. 'Gosh, I hope this is the last one.' David sighed.

Dear David

This is the last letter I have written please believe me. I am glad you managed to get through the funeral, I just want to say well done, as I know it cannot have been easy and hopefully now you have laid me to rest, you can get on with your life. I am so sorry it is not with me. Again, I did make several attempts to tell you of my illness, but the longer it went on the harder it became.

Enjoy the rest of your life with Adam, I am just sorry it won't include me. I am sure I will forever be in your thoughts, but if you do forget me some days, please don't beat yourself up. I do not want you to feel guilty if you find another good woman to look after you as I have done for the past fifteen years, I wouldn't want you missing out, please do not feel as though you are committing adultery, as you are not, sadly I am gone and I don't want you to be alone forever in this world. This just leaves me to say, bye, bye until we meet again in the next world.

XXXX

David stood crying, he thanked Lorraine and gathered everyone together and announced that he was about to make a toast. David toasted a glass to Joan and thanked her for being such a wonderful wife, mother to Adam, work colleague and friend to everyone and asked that they all joined him in raising their glasses in memory of Joan. Everyone raised their glasses and said Joan, through their tears.

David was startled by a tap on the shoulder and turned sharply to see a rather shy girl standing there with her hand held out.

'Hi, I am Laura.' Laura turned a rather bright shade of red.

'Hi, Laura. I don't think I have met you before. How did you know Joan?' David asked innocently.

'Well, this is rather embarrassing really.' Laura struggled to find the words. 'I only met her a couple of months ago at a singles meeting.'

'Oh my gosh, please don't tell me this is another secret my wife had.' David almost fell over. 'Was she gay also?' David was talking through gritted teeth.

'No, I am not gay and neither was your wife.' Laura reassured. 'I recently lost my husband to this awful disease. Joan and I used to meet regularly and offer comfort to each other and then Joan asked me to keep an eye on you after her passing.'

'Oh, my this is too much for one day.' David sniffed.

'I am sorry, I will leave you alone, I was unsure how you would take the news, but Joan was very insistent that I attend the funeral and speak to you during the wake.' Laura was unable to look David in the eye.

'Oh please, no Laura, this is not your fault. I don't want you to feel uncomfortable, just that Joan has arranged my whole life for me and I had no idea that she was ill or dying.' David placed a reassuring hand on her shoulder.

'She was an extremely brave lady; I only had the pleasure of knowing her for a couple of months, yet you had the pleasure of being married to her for fifteen years, she must have been an amazing wife.' Laura was feeling less awkward now and felt brave enough to hand David the letter Joan had written and given her instructions to pass to David at the funeral.

Dear David

Please believe me this is the final letter. I was concerned that you will spend the rest of your days moping around and never look at another lady again, so I decided to visit a single's club for widowed ladies. As you can expect that most of the ladies there thought I was insane and a rather sick (as our son would say), that I wasn't even dead and I was looking for a companion for you after my passing. The only lady there that gave me any attention was Laura, this delightful lady that is standing before you. She has recently lost her husband to this awful disease and she was willing to become a friend, so much that I believe she will make a fantastic and supportive friend for you. David, I don't want you spending the rest of your life living in the past, please try and move on. I am not trying to marry you off, besides you have only just buried me today, but I do believe it will do you both the world of good having some company. Thank Laura for the couple of months we had together and it is a real shame I never met her earlier in my life, she is a truly wonderful lady. Again, I just wish to say, thank you for a wonderful life and marriage and take good care of Adam, which I have no doubt you will. Until we meet again, yours Joan xxxxx.

'Well I am gob smacked, what can I say?' David started twisting his tie anxiously around his fingers.

'I am sorry this is a bad time.' Laura turned to leave.

David called after her. 'No Laura, please wait' David gestured towards an empty table. 'Please come and join me, I don't want you feeling like this is your fault'.

'Thank you, David' Laura smiled and followed David to the empty table.

Afterword

Thank you for purchasing and reading this book.

My inspiration came from, having lost so many people to this awful disease. My thoughts started about; how do different people, deal with the news in their way.

Other books by

Kathleen Kirkland

Mum Runners Florida Vacation – adult fiction.

Available in paperback through your local bookstore, or on E-Book.

Samantha, Suzie and Sharon, new best friends after training and running the London Marathon together, are off on holiday to Florida with their families.

The holiday brings, lots and lots of laughter and many, many tears. The main reason for the holiday is Brett proposed to Suzie as she crossed the finishing line of the London Marathon. The thirteen of them, hire a villa together for ten days, what can possibly, go wrong?

Other books by

Kath Kirkland

The Chocolate Thief – junior read. Available in

paperback through your local bookstore, or on E-Book.

Billy likes chocolate. All he eats is chocolate. A chocolate thief starts stealing all the chocolate in the town. Billy is accused of the thefts by his classmates, the head-teacher and even the police.

Who is the chocolate thief and will Billy be able to eat chocolate again?

Will the police catch the chocolate thief who is destroying the lives of many children?

How to contact Kathleen

If you have any questions for Kathleen, you can contact her in several ways or follow her on Social Media.

Sign up to the newsletter -
https://mailchi.mp/91f8e6d1c5d0/kath-kirklands-newsletter

Email –
kathkirklandauthor@gmail.com

Twitter –
@kathauthor

Facebook –
https://www.facebook.com/kathkirklandauthor/

Instagram –
https://www.instagram.com/kmkauthor/

LinkedIn –
https://www.linkedin.com/in/kathkirklandauthor/

Kathleen is free for book readings and book signings and to attend events and club meetings. Please contact her for details.

www.ingramcontent.com/pod-product-compliance
Lightning Source LLC
Chambersburg PA
CBHW060958050726
47592CB00003B/1257